BABY SITTERS LITTLE SISTER

Karen's Ghost

BABY SITTERS

LITTLE SISTER

Karen's Ghost

ANN M. MARTIN

ILLUSTRATIONS BY HEATHER BURNS

SCHOLASTIC INC.

For Paula

Copyright © 1990 by Ann M. Martin

This book was originally published in paperback in 1990.

All rights reserved. Published by Scholastic Inc., *Publishers since 1920.* SCHOLASTIC, THE BABY-SITTERS LITTLE SISTER, and associated logos are trademarks and/or registered trademarks of Scholastic Inc.

The publisher does not have any control over and does not assume any responsibility for author or third-party websites or their content.

No part of this publication may be reproduced, stored in a retrieval system, or transmitted in any form or by any means, electronic, mechanical, photocopying, recording, or otherwise, without written permission of the publisher. For information regarding permission, write to Scholastic Inc., Attention: Permissions Department, 557 Broadway, New York, NY 10012.

This book is a work of fiction. Names, characters, places, and incidents are either the product of the author's imagination or are used fictitiously, and any resemblance to actual persons, living or dead, business establishments, events, or locales is entirely coincidental.

ISBN 978-1-338-81512-2

10 9 8 7 6 5 4 3 2 1   23 24 25 26 27

Printed in the U.S.A. 40
This edition first printing 2023

Book design by Maeve Norton

CHAPTER 1

Kristy, do I really have to go to sleep now?" I asked my big sister.

"Yes, you do. It's already past your bedtime."

I sighed. Kristy is one of my favorite people in the whole wide world. But she is thirteen. And when she says to do something, you have to do it. Besides, Kristy was my baby-sitter that night. And you have to listen to baby-sitters, just like you have to listen to teachers and mommies and daddies and grandparents and policemen.

"One more story?" I begged.

Kristy shook her head. "You already had one more story. And before that you had three stories."

"Yeah," I said, smiling. "And all of them were about Halloween."

"Are you going to be able to sleep tonight?" Kristy asked me.

"Sure," I replied. "Witches and ghosts don't scare me." (That was easy to say when the light was on and Kristy was sitting next to me.)

"All right," said Kristy. She sounded a little uncertain. "Under the covers, then. I hope you have good dreams tonight."

Kristy stood up, and I slid under my covers. I scrunched up my pillow.

"Don't forget to turn on my night-light," I said.

Kristy switched on my special light from Disney World. Then she kissed me good night, turned off my lamp, and headed for the door.

"Leave the door open a crack!" I called.

"Okay." Kristy left my room.

I was alone.

I looked around. I was glad the night-light was on and the door was open.

Halloween was coming. That was why I wanted to hear all the Halloween stories. I just love Halloween. I love ghosts and witches, too. But I will tell you something. They *do* scare me a little bit. But that is only because a real witch lives next door. And a ghost lives upstairs and haunts his room on the third floor of our house. He haunts the attic, too.

The witch is named Morbidda Destiny. Well, that's what *I* call her. It's her witch name. Most people call her Mrs. Porter, but they don't know anything. Morbidda Destiny holds witch meetings at her house. At night, she flies around on a broomstick. (Adults do not believe this.)

I sat up and looked out my window. Morbidda Destiny's broomstick was leaning next to her front door. I could see it by the porch light. I guessed she wasn't going to go out haunting that night.

I lay down again. I listened.

CREEEEAK. What was that? Was it Ben Brewer?

I felt gigundo scared. Ben Brewer is the ghost in my house. I am not sure if he ever drifts below the third floor. What if he does? What if he was in my room *right then* . . . watching me?

"Go away, Ben Brewer," I whispered. "You can't scare me."

CREEEEAK.

"Honest," I said. "You can't scare me." But my voice was shaking.

I sat up and checked out the window again.

Morbidda Destiny's porch light was off! Was her broom still there? Was she out haunting?

I almost called for Kristy. Then I remembered that I had told her that witches and ghosts don't scare me.

I tried to think about other things. First I thought about Kristy. She is actually my *step-sister*. That's because my daddy married her mommy. See, I have two families. . . .

CHAPTER 2

I think I am lucky to have two families. Most people have just one. Some people do not have any at all. That is so, so sad.

I am Karen Brewer. I just turned seven years old. I have blonde hair and blue eyes and some freckles. I wear glasses. I even have two pairs. One pair is for reading and the other pair is for the rest of the time. (Well, I do not have to wear glasses in bed at night. But I have to put them on when I get up in the morning.)

I have a little brother. His name is Andrew. He is almost five. Most of the time, Andrew and I live with Mommy and Seth. Seth is our step-father. Mommy and Seth live in a little house. Seth has a dog named Midgie and a cat named

Rocky. I have a rat named Emily Junior. Seth is a very nice stepfather.

But Andrew and I have another house and another family. That is the big house (a mansion) where Daddy lives. See, a long time ago, when I was still in preschool, Mommy and Daddy got divorced. Later, they each got married again. Mommy married Seth, and Daddy married Elizabeth. Elizabeth is my stepmother. It is a good thing Daddy has such a big house because Elizabeth has four children. They are Charlie and Sam, who are in high school; David Michael, who is seven like me; and Kristy. Sam, Charlie, and David Michael are my stepbrothers. Kristy is my stepsister.

Guess what. I also have a little sister. Daddy and Elizabeth adopted her. She was born in a country called Vietnam. She is just two years old. We named her Emily Michelle. And I love her so much I named my rat after her.

Another person lives at the big house. That is Nannie, Elizabeth's mother. She takes care of

Emily Michelle while Daddy and Elizabeth are at work and everyone else is at school. Doesn't Daddy have a big family? It's even bigger when Andrew and I come to stay. We live at Daddy's every other weekend and for two weeks during the summer.

Oh, there are also two pets at the big house. One is Shannon, David Michael's puppy. The other is Boo-Boo, Daddy's fat old cat. I have never liked Boo-Boo very much. He scratches if you are not careful.

The big house is the one with the witch next door and the ghost upstairs. It is a scary place around Halloween. Even so, I am glad I have two houses and two families. It is fun. Andrew and I have two of almost everything. We each have two bicycles, one at the little house and one at the big house. I have two stuffed cats, one at each house. I even have a piece of Tickly, my special blanket, at each house. Plus, Andrew and I have clothes and toys and almost every-thing at each house. That way, we hardly have to pack when we go back and forth between Mommy's and Daddy's.

Since we have two of so many things, I call myself Karen Two-Two and I call my brother Andrew Two-Two. Those names came from a book that Ms. Colman read to our class. It was called *Jacob Two-Two Meets the Hooded Fang.* (Ms. Colman is my second-grade teacher at Stoneybrook Academy.)

Oh. I almost forgot. I even have two best

friends. Hannie Papadakis is my big-house best friend. She lives across the street from Daddy and one house down. Nancy Dawes is my little-house best friend. She lives next door to Mommy. Hannie and Nancy and I call ourselves the Three Musketeers. We are all in Ms. Colman's class.

Being a two-two is pretty okay, I thought, as my eyes started to close.

I forgot about witches and ghosts, and fell asleep.

CHAPTER 3

By the next morning I had forgotten about Morbidda Destiny and Ben Brewer. Sort of. What I was thinking about was Halloween.

As soon as breakfast was over, I said to David Michael and Andrew, "Let's plan our Halloween costumes."

"Okay," said the boys.

We went to the playroom, where we have lots of dress-up clothes.

Emily Michelle followed us.

"Go away, Emily," said David Michael. "Halloween is for big kids. You're too little."

I could tell that Emily had not understood him.

"Play," she said. Only it sounded more like "pway" or "pray."

"She just wants to play with the toys," I told my brothers. "Let her stay."

"Okay," said David Michael. But he looked like he thought it was a bad idea.

My brothers and I began to pull things out of the dress-up box. We found some pretty neat stuff. Daddy buys us costumes sometimes. He knows we like to pretend. We found hats and a wand and a tiara and a cowboy suit and fireman's boots and more.

"I'm going to be a cowboy," said Andrew, after he had looked at everything.

"I don't think the cowboy suit fits you," I told him. "It's too big."

Andrew tried the pants on and they slid right off.

"Maybe next year," I said. "Next year you can be a cowboy."

"Yeah," replied Andrew sadly.

"Hey, I know! I'm going to be a Teenage

Mutant Ninja Turtle!" cried David Michael. "Just like on TV."

"We don't have a Teenage Mutant Ninja Turtle costume," I pointed out.

"Maybe Mom will help me make one," said David Michael. "What about you, Karen? What do you want to be?"

I looked at all the stuff we had tossed on the floor. "Usually I dress up as a witch," I said. "Maybe I should be something different this year. Maybe a beauty queen or a princess. Or Raggedy Ann. That might be fun."

"Me! Yook!" cried Emily suddenly.

My brothers and I had not been paying attention to Emily. When we looked at her, we saw that she had put on high heels, a big straw hat, a feather boa, and a tutu. We could not help laughing a little.

Then Emily laughed, too. "Funny!" she said.

"You know, she does look pretty cute," said David Michael.

"Yeah," agreed Andrew and I.

"Maybe," said David Michael slowly, "if we
get a costume for her and bring her along with
us when we trick-or-treat, people will give us
more candy."

"Yeah!" exclaimed Andrew and I.

But then I stopped and thought about something. "You know," I said at last, "Emily is only
two. Well, two and a half. She doesn't under-
stand about Halloween. She *is* too little. Just
like you said, David Michael."

"Oh, forget that. That was before I saw Emily dressed up. Now, what should her costume be?" he wondered.

"Maybe *she* could be a witch this year," I suggested.

"Nah. She has to be cute," said David Michael.

"A princess?" suggested Andrew.

David Michael nodded slowly. "Yes. . . . I think a princess would be perfect. Now, what about us?"

We just couldn't decide. And we still hadn't decided by the time Hannie Papadakis called up and invited me over to her house.

CHAPTER 4

I went over to Hannie's after lunch. I am always careful when I cross the street. I look both ways and make sure no cars are coming. I do that before I even step off the curb. Then I run to Hannie's.

When I rang the Papadakises' bell, Linny answered the door. He is Hannie's big brother. He and David Michael are friends.

"Hannie!" he yelled. "Your Musketeer is here!"

Ever since Linny found out that Hannie and Nancy and I are the Three Musketeers, that is all he calls us. He is a pain.

"Karen!" Hannie called. "Come on upstairs."

I ignored Linny. I ran to Hannie's room.

"Let's talk about Halloween costumes," I said, as soon as I got there.

"*I* already know what I'm going to be," said Hannie. "I am going to be a bride. I am going to wear my bridal dress from when I married Scott Hsu."

(Hannie is the only second-grader I know who is married. She had a wedding not long ago. She wore her mother's wedding dress and she married Scott, this boy down the street. I was the bridesmaid.)

"I don't know what my costume will be," I said. "I don't think I will dress up as a witch again."

"How about a cat?" suggested Hannie.

I shook my head.

"A rat? You could be Emily Junior."

I shook my head.

Then we both thought for awhile.

"I know!" I cried. "I will dress up as Old Ben Brewer. As his ghost."

17

"But then you'd just wear a regular old ghost costume," said Hannie. "That isn't special."

"It will be to me. *I* will know that *I* am Ben Brewer."

"Tell me about Ben Brewer again," said Hannie. "Put all your stories together into one big story."

"Okay," I replied. "I'll tell you as much as I know."

I drew in a deep breath. "Old Ben Brewer

was as unusual as anything," I began. "He ate fried dandelions —"

"And he never left the house," added Hannie.

"Right," I said. "Well, that was when he was old. When he was young, he was just like everybody else. He got married, and he and his wife had a son, Jeremy. Jeremy was my grandfather, only I never knew him. He died before I was born.

"Anyway, when Ben became an old man and he was living alone in our big house, a ghost began to haunt him. He would come to Ben's bedroom at midnight. Ben did everything he could to keep the ghost away, but the ghost always got in. You know how ghosts are. The ghost would come down the chimney or even walk right through a wall or the door. There was no way to escape that ghost." (I had heard bits and pieces of the rest of this story from Daddy and other people.)

"Why did the ghost haunt Ben?" asked Hannie.

"I don't know," I replied.

"And how did Ben Brewer become a ghost himself?"

"I don't know that, either."

Hannie looked disappointed. We began talking about our Halloween costumes again.

CHAPTER 5

Ms. Colman is the best teacher I have ever had. For one thing, she hardly ever yells. She never makes you feel stupid. She always listens to you. And she is patient with me. See, I am the youngest kid in my class because I skipped. So sometimes I forget to use my indoor voice or to wear my glasses. Ms. Colman reminds me nicely.

Another thing I like about Ms. Colman is that she is always making Surprising Announcements. For instance, on the Monday after my weekend at the big house, she said, "Class, I have an announcement."

Ms. Colman was smiling, so I knew it would be a good announcement. I looked at Ricky

Torres, who was sitting next to me. Ricky and I and another girl (Natalie Springer) all wear glasses. So we all sit in the front row. Ricky and I grinned at each other. Then I turned around and glanced at the back row, where Nancy Dawes and Hannie were sitting. The three of us grinned, too. (I used to sit with Hannie and Nancy. That was before I got my glasses.)

As I turned to face the front again, I caught

Pamela's eye. Pamela Harding is a new girl. I do not like her and she does not like me.

I almost stuck my tongue out at Pamela, but I remembered that I should act like other second-graders.

Anyway, Ms. Colman began to make her Surprising Announcement.

"Class," she said, "as you know, Halloween is on a Saturday this year. So we will have a class Halloween party on the Friday afternoon before Halloween."

"Yay!" shouted the kids in my class.

Ms. Colman smiled. Then she went on. "We will have refreshments and you can wear your costumes, of course. We'll play some games, but then we will . . ." Ms. Colman paused.

I drew in my breath. We will *what*? I wondered.

"We will turn off the overhead light and sit in a circle and tell scary stories. Anyone who wants to may tell a story."

Oh, boy! All around me, kids were saying things like, "Cool!" and, "I can't wait!" and, "I know the *best* story!"

Ricky said to me, "I am going to tell the story about the man whose eyeballs fell out and walked around by themselves."

"That is so gross," I replied.

Ricky just laughed. "Hey!" he called to one of his friends. "I am going to tell the story about the walking eyeballs!"

Well, I knew what scary story *I* was going to tell. I was going to tell the Ben Brewer story, of course. It would be the best of all the scary stories. Ms. Colman had not said we were going to have a storytelling contest, but I wanted to tell the best story anyway.

"Hey, Karen," called a voice.

I turned around. It was Pamela Harding. Gigundo yuck.

"What?" I replied.

"What story are *you* going to tell?" she asked.

"Secret," I said.

"I bet you don't have a story at all."

"I do too. What story are *you* going to tell?"

"Secret." Pamela smiled smugly.

"Then I bet *you* don't have a story."

Pamela's face turned red. "I do, too. And it will be the very best one."

Ha. We would see about that.

CHAPTER 6

After school that day, Nancy came over to my house. We went to my room and took Emily Junior out of her cage. We let her run around in the special rat playground that Andrew and Seth made for my seventh birthday.

"Let's try out scary stories," Nancy said to me. "What's the scariest thing that ever happened to you?"

"Getting lost at Disney World," I replied. "But that's not the story I am going to tell. The story I am going to tell is a ghost story. It is much scarier than telling about getting lost at Disney World."

"Are you going to tell about Ben Brewer?" asked Nancy, wide-eyed.

I nodded. Nancy had heard several Ben Brewer stories. They always scared her out of her wits.

"What story are you going to tell?" I asked Nancy.

Nancy frowned.

"You *are* going to tell a story, aren't you?"

"Well, of course," replied Nancy.

I should have known. Nancy loves to be the center of attention. She plans to be an actress when she grows up.

"Let's see," said Nancy slowly. "Okay. Once — you know my charm bracelet? The one with the horse and all the other animals on it?"

"Yeah."

"Well, once I lost the bracelet. And you know what? A leprechaun had *stolen* it. . . . Honest," she added when she saw my face.

"How do you know?" I asked.

"Because I found it in my underwear drawer, and I *never* keep it there."

"Hmmm," I said.

"Not scary enough?" asked Nancy.

"I don't think so," I replied. "Tell me another."

Nancy told *two* more stories. They were not scary.

"Tell me a Ben Brewer story," said Nancy at last.

"Okay." I told Nancy just what I had told Hannie on Saturday. I told her all the Ben Brewer stories in one. I said how Ben was haunted by a ghost in his old age, and how he haunts the big house now. Especially the attic and his room on the third floor.

"But who was haunting Ben?" Nancy wanted to know.

"I'm not sure."

"And *why* was a ghost haunting Ben? There must have been a reason."

"Yeah. . . . And another thing," I went on. "Why did Ben become a ghost? Boy, I better work on this story."

"Why?" asked Nancy.

"Because I've got to tell the scariest story of all. I have to show Pamela Harding that I know a story and it's a good one."

"Pamela," said Nancy, "is not the only other person who will be listening to your ghost story. And anyway, this is not a contest."

"I know, I know," I replied. "But I still want a good story. The *best* story. I'm sorry, but I do. And right now, this story is not finished. We have too many questions about it. I will have to find out what happened to Ben Brewer and why he was haunted."

"Oh, just make something up," said Nancy.

"No, I think a *true* ghost story will be scarier. Don't you?"

"Yes," Nancy replied, and shivered. She paused. "A true ghost story . . ."

"Ooh," was all I said. I felt a little scared.

CHAPTER 7

After awhile, Nancy said she had to go home. We took Emily Junior out of the playground and put her back in her cage. Then Nancy left.

I found Mommy and Andrew in the kitchen. Mommy was making dinner and Andrew was helping. He was stirring something in a bowl at the table. He was standing on a chair, wearing an apron. The apron reached down to his feet.

I giggled. He looked funny.

Then I said, "Mommy?"

"Yes?" Mommy turned away from the stove to look at me.

"Remember when you and Daddy were still married?"

"Yes." Mommy looked a little nervous. Sometimes I ask her to marry Daddy again. She does not like to talk about that.

"And you and Daddy and Andrew and I lived in the big house?"

"Yes," said Mommy again.

"Well, when you lived in the big house, did you ever see Ben Brewer's ghost?"

"Karen —" Mommy began.

And then *Andrew* started to looked nervous. He stopped his stirring.

"Or do you know anything *about* Ben Brewer?" I went on.

"He was just a lonely old man," Mommy told me.

"No. That's not true," I replied. "I mean, maybe he *was* lonely, but he was haunted by a ghost, too."

"The one that could come down his chimney?" said Andrew. His eyes had grown huge.

"Yes," I said.

"Karen, those are just stories," Mommy told me.

"How did they start?" I asked. "Huh? How did they start?" I sat at the kitchen table, crossed my arms, and looked at Mommy.

"The way most silly stories start," she answered. She sat down at the table, too, and pulled Andrew onto her lap. "People think someone is a little odd, so they make up stories about why he's odd. Your great-grandfather was a recluse. Do you know what that means?"

"That he wrecked things?" suggested Andrew.

"No, silly," I said. "*I* know what a recluse is. It's a person who stays inside all the time and won't come out."

"Right," said Mommy. "And that's all that was wrong with Ben Brewer. Except for the fried dandelions. I think that's true, too. And that's as strange as being a recluse. So people made up stories about your poor great-grandfather."

"Are you *sure*?" I asked.

"*Yes*," said Mommy.

"Then why won't Boo-Boo go near the third floor at the big house?" I asked her. I felt pleased with myself.

"Because he's lazy," said Mommy. She put Andrew back on his chair and returned to her cooking.

"No," I said. "It's because he knows about the ghost of old Ben. Animals can sense those things. Boo-Boo is afraid."

"He's a 'fraidy-cat," said Andrew, giggling.

I made a face. "You guys aren't taking this seriously. I am going to call Kristy," I said. "She will help me find out the true ghost story. . . . Can I call Kristy?" I asked Mommy.

"Sure," she answered.

I knew that Mommy didn't think Kristy and I would find out anything about Ben Brewer. But *I* knew better.

I called the big house. Kristy answered the phone! That was a good sign. I told her what I wanted to do.

"Will you help me?" I asked her.

"Of course," she replied. "Come over tomorrow after school. We will do some detective work."

CHAPTER 8

The next afternoon, my big stepbrother Charlie came to the little house to pick me up. He has his own car and he is very proud of it. Then Charlie drove me back to the big house. Kristy met me at the front door.

"Hi!" I cried. "Thank you, Charlie! Okay, Kristy. Let's get to work."

Kristy has as much energy as I do. "Ready when you are," she replied.

The only thing I could think to do was to look at some old books in the library. Not in the public library. In the room Daddy and Elizabeth *call* the library, where they keep their books. Daddy collects old-fashioned ones. They are so old that their pages are yellow and they smell funny.

"Let's start in the library," I said.

"Okay," agreed Kristy.

We went straight to the oldest of the old books. Some of the books were about Stoneybrook a long time ago. We looked at those first.

"Guess what!" I exclaimed. "They used to spell the name of our town wrong. They spelled it like this: S-t-o-n-e-y-b-r-o-o-k-e. They put an extra 'e' on the end."

"I don't think it was wrong," said Kristy.

"That was just the way the name was spelled a long time ago."

"Oh," I said.

Kristy and I looked at the history books. They were hard to read and we could not find anything about my great-grandfather.

Then suddenly Kristy cried, "Hey, look! A genealogy!"

"A what?" I said.

"A genealogy. That's a book that tells about the people in a family. And here is the Brewer genealogy. Old Ben must be in here."

Guess what. He was! We found him toward the back of the book. But we didn't find much information.

"All it says," Kristy told me, "is the date Ben was born; the names of his parents; the date he got married; the name of his wife; when they had Jeremy, their son — he would be your grandfather — and the dates when Ben and his wife died."

"That isn't very helpful, is it?" I said.

"No." Kristy looked disappointed.

"You know what?" I said shakily. "I don't think we're going to find anything here. We are going to have to go into Ben's bedroom."

CHAPTER 9

Into Ben Brewer's *bed*room?" cried Kristy. "Oh, Karen . . ."

"We went in the attic once," I reminded her. "We thought the attic was haunted, but nothing happened. Except that David Michael played a trick on us."

"Yeah," said Kristy, smiling. "He hid, and we thought he had disappeared. But nothing bad happened. Still, Ben's bedroom . . ."

We had to go, though. We could not think of any other way to find out more about Ben. Well, I guess we could have called Daddy at his office, but I did not think he would like that.

Kristy and I held hands. Bravely we walked

to the second floor. Bravely we walked to the third floor. Bravely we walked down the hallway to Ben Brewer's bedroom. We stood in front of the closed door. We did not feel so brave anymore.

"I wish the door was open," said Kristy. "Then we could see inside."

"Maybe it's locked!" I said hopefully.

"Maybe," replied Kristy.

I turned the handle. The door opened easily. "Here goes," I said.

Very, very slowly Kristy and I walked inside the room.

"Pew! Gigundo pew!" I said. "This place smells."

"It's just musty," said Kristy. "It has been shut up for a long time. It's dusty and the air is stale."

We tiptoed around the room. Some of the furniture was covered with sheets. What was not covered looked so, so old. And messy.

"Ben Brewer wasn't very neat, was he?" I said.

"Not at all," agreed Kristy.

There was stuff everywhere — old newspapers, candles, books, clothes, a clock on the mantelpiece over the fireplace.

"You know what I think?" I said. "I think this is exactly the way Ben's room looked when he died. No one has touched it in years and years," I added dramatically.

"Hey," whispered Kristy. "There's the

fireplace the ghost came down." (Kristy knew the stories as well as I did.)

Kristy and I peered into the fireplace. It looked like a regular old fireplace. The bricks were black from Ben's fires, and it was filled with ashes. That was all.

Kristy and I did not feel so scared anymore. We let go of each other's hands and we walked around the room by ourselves. We poked into things. We looked under sheets and on bookcases.

Kristy had just said, "Well, I guess there's nothing here," when I let out a scream.

"What? What's the matter?" Kristy ran to my side.

"Look what I found," I said.

It was a book. I had opened a drawer in a table by Ben's bed. I had seen a tiny knob inside. When I touched it, another drawer — a secret one — had sprung out from the back. And in that drawer was a diary. I opened it. I saw the name Jeremy Brewer. I flipped through the book to see what I could learn, but Jeremy's handwriting was hard to read, so I gave the book to Kristy to look at.

What I had found was the story of Ben Brewer. Or most of it.

"It's here," Kristy whispered. "Ben's son Jeremy kept a diary, and the story is *here*."

Just from reading a few pages, Kristy knew we had found a gigundo spooky story. And the spookiest thing about it was that it was true. It had to be. Diaries are always true . . . aren't they?

I grabbed the book with one hand and Kristy with the other.

We ran all the way downstairs to Kristy's bedroom.

CHAPTER 10

Oh, my gosh. Oh, my gosh," I kept saying as Kristy and I looked through the diary. Sometimes I said, "Ooh, scary."

This is the story we found, the story that Jeremy wrote down about his father, Old Ben Brewer.

Guess what? Ben's birthday was on Halloween. Can you imagine? A Halloween birthday. I would not like that. First of all, you would probably only get to have one party, a Halloween birthday party, instead of a Halloween party *and* a birthday party. And second, who would want to be born on the scariest day of the year?

Then we found out that every ten years, at

midnight on Halloween, Ben gives himself a birthday party.

"A *haunted* birthday," I said to Kristy. My teeth began to chatter. That is how scared I was.

"Yeah," said Kristy. She looked nervous. "Jeremy writes that the birthday parties started *after* his father died."

"What happens at the haunted birthday parties?" I asked Kristy. I was letting her read most of the diary. Jeremy wrote in cursive, and I am not very good at reading cursive yet. It takes a long time.

"Let me see," said Kristy. She flipped through the book. Then she looked again. "I can't find anything," she said at last. "I would probably have to read the whole diary. From beginning to end. That would take awhile."

"I bet that at a haunted birthday party," I said, "Ben invites his ghost friends over and they eat ghost cake. Maybe he invites Morbidda Destiny, too. I wonder if there are other ghosts *in our house* who come to the —"

"Yikes!" shrieked Kristy.

"What?" I asked.

"*This* Halloween, Ben is going to have one of his parties! It's the tenth year. Oh, no. I don't believe it!"

"Are you *sure*?" I asked Kristy.

"Positive." She read to me from the book. She was right.

Suddenly it was my turn to shriek. (Again.) "I'm going to be *here* this Halloween!" I exclaimed. "I will be at the big house. Halloween is a big-house weekend for Andrew and me. I will be here for a haunted birthday party." I was scared — but I was also excited. My story for the Halloween party was getting better and better, but there were still some things I did not know.

I did not know why Ben was haunted when he was alive. I did not know who had haunted him. I did not know why he became a ghost after he died. But if I could not find out those things, I *could* make them up. I did not want to, but I could.

Now I knew for sure that my story would be better than Pamela Harding's.

"Do you want to take the diary home with you when your mother picks you up?" Kristy asked me a little later.

I looked at the diary. It was so spooky. I almost said, "No." Then I changed my mind.

"Yes," I said. "Maybe if I try very hard, I can read Jeremy Brewer's cursive writing. And if I read the diary carefully, I might find the answers to some of my questions. We did not read the diary very carefully today."

"No," agreed Kristy. "We didn't."

She handed me the diary. She looked relieved.

Honk, honk! Mommy was here. It was time to go back to the little house.

CHAPTER 11

I thanked Kristy. I called good-bye to Nannie and Charlie and Emily and David Michael. Then I ran outside.

I climbed into Mommy's car and buckled my seat belt. The diary was in my hand. And in that diary was the best story ever.

"What's that?" asked Andrew. He peered over the front seat.

"Oh, just an old diary," I said.

"Whose old diary?" asked Mommy.

"What's a diary?" asked Andrew.

"It's Jeremy Brewer's diary," I told Mommy. "Ben's son. And," I added, turning to Andrew, "a diary is a book that you write in. You tell about things that happen to you, or things that happen with your family and friends. It is a very private thing."

"Then how come you have someone else's diary?" Andrew wanted to know.

"Because the guy is dead now. He won't care if I read his diary."

"Karen," said Mommy," 'the guy' is your grandfather. Be nice about him. And how did you get his diary?"

"We found it in Ben Brewer's room. It was in a secret drawer in the table next to his bed.

Kristy and I were so sc — I mean, so brave. We marched right into that room and we searched it until we found this diary. Jeremy must have wanted to tell the story of his father. I guess that's why he put the diary in his father's room. Anyway, did you know that Ben's birthday was on Halloween? And after he died he started giving himself haunted birthday parties."

"Oh, Karen," said Mommy.

"It's true. That's what Jeremy wrote."

"Really?" said Andrew. His bottom lip trembled.

"Really," I told him. "He gives one every ten years. And guess what. *This* Halloween he'll be giving a haunted party and *we* will be at the big house for it. It will happen at midnight."

Andrew began to cry. "No!" he wailed. "Then I'm not going to Daddy's for Halloween. I don't want the ghosts to get me."

"Andrew," said Mommy, "there are no ghosts. Besides, you will be asleep at midnight, so you don't need to worry. And Karen, you are scaring your brother. Please stop it right now."

"Okay," I replied. But I sat back in my seat and said softly, "Yup. Every ten years. A haunted party. A haunted birthday party. At midnight."

Mommy stopped the car. She turned around in her seat. "Karen, that is enough. I just told you that you are scaring Andrew. I don't want to hear another word out of you until we get home. And then I want you to go to your room for fifteen minutes and think about what you've done."

I began to cry. In the front seat, Andrew was crying, too. We cried all the way home. Mommy did not say anything.

At home, I spent fifteen minutes in my room playing with Emily Junior. I tried to think about what I'd done. But all I could think about was Ben.

When the fifteen minutes were over, Mommy said I could come out. She said it was

dinnertime. I ate my whole dinner without saying anything about Ben or Jeremy or the diary.

Mommy gave me a hug and a kiss. I was glad
she was not mad at me anymore. But *I* was mad
at *Andrew.* He had gotten me in trouble because
he is a crybaby. So when we were alone I sang
to him, *"Haunted birthday to you, haunted birthday to
you. Ben Brewer will get you. Haunted birthday
to you."*

Do you know what? Andrew stuck his
tongue out at me.

CHAPTER 12

On a Friday afternoon when there was still a week and a day left before Halloween, Ms. Colman let us make decorations for our classroom. We sat wherever we wanted and we made paper pumpkins and witches and skeletons and black cats and ghosts.

Ricky and I took our chairs to the back of the room and sat with Hannie and Nancy. Ricky was making a skeleton. He worked very hard on it. He cut out the arms and legs separately so that they could move. Hannie was making a grinning pumpkin. She called it a jack-o'-lantern. Nancy was making a black cat. And I was making — what else? — a ghost.

"Well, I have decided what I'm going to be

for Halloween," Ricky said. He was cutting busily.

"You have? What?" I asked.

"A gas station person."

Hannie and Nancy and I glanced at each other.

"Hmm," I said. "Interesting."

"What are you going to be, Karen?" asked Ricky.

"The ghost of Ben Brewer."

We kept on talking about costumes. Suddenly I had a great idea.

"Hey!" I exclaimed, "Ricky, you and Nancy should come trick-or-treating with Hannie and me. We're going out with my brother and my stepbrother and my little sister."

"And Scott," added Hannie.

"Oh, yeah. Your husband," said Ricky.

"But not my brother. Linnie won't go trick-or-treating with any girls."

"You know what else?" I went on. "If we all go together, we should go as characters from a movie or something. That would be really cool."

"Yeah!" said the others, except for Hannie.

"Do you think your parents will let you come trick-or-treating in our neighborhood?" I asked Nancy and Ricky. "My big sister will come with us. Kristy is a baby-sitter. Your parents would not have to worry."

"I think so," said Nancy and Ricky at the same time.

"Great! Now. What should we dress up as?" I asked.

"How about the kids from Peanuts?" said Nancy. But nobody wanted to be Charlie Brown.

"How about Superheroes?" said Ricky.

"Nah," said Hannie.

"*I* know!" I cried. "*The Wizard of Oz*. We could have a Dorothy and a Tinman and a Wicked Witch of the West and everything. There would be lots of neat costumes."

"I want to be the Scarecrow," said Ricky, looking excited.

"I want to be Dorothy," said Nancy. "She's the star."

"Perfect," I said. "I'll be the Wicked Witch of the West. I already have a witch costume."

"I still want to be a bride," said Hannie.

We talked it over and decided that was okay. Then we thought about who the others could be. This is what we decided: Scott — the Tinman; David Michael — the Lion; Andrew — Toto;

and Emily — a Munchkin. We hoped they would like our idea. *We* thought it was great.

But someone else did not.

"What a stupid plan," said Pamela Harding. She must have been listening. "You guys are such babies. *My* friends and I are going to be waitresses and cheerleaders and punk rockers. We will be much more grown-up."

"We'll just see about that," I told Pamela. Then I ignored her.

CHAPTER 13

Three more days! Three more days!" I sang.

It was Wednesday. The next day would be Thursday. That would just be a regular day. Then would come Friday, the day of our class Halloween party. And *then* would come . . . Halloween.

Guess what? Everyone liked our idea to go trick-or-treating as characters from *The Wizard of Oz*. No one even wanted to switch costumes. I thought David Michael might say, "*I* want to be the Tinman, not the raggedy old Lion." But he did not.

So on Wednesday after school, Mommy was helping Andrew and me with our costumes. My costume was easy. I just had to add some things to my regular witch costume so that I would look like the Wicked Witch of the West. But Andrew's costume was hard.

"Toto!" Mommy had exclaimed when I told her what Andrew was going to dress up as. "Where are we going to get a dog costume?"

"Not just a dog costume," Andrew spoke up. "A Toto costume. I have to look like Toto. He is a certain kind of dog."

In the end, Mommy had to make Andrew's costume all by herself. We went shopping. We found material that looked like dark fur. We found a little dog nose. We even found a book that explained how to make whiskers. Andrew's costume was going to be great.

That afternoon Mommy was finishing Toto's head. Andrew was helping. He was making the whiskers. I was working on my witch shoes.

When the doorbell rang, I said, "I'll get it! I think it's Nancy. She said she would wear her Dorothy costume over."

I ran to the door and opened it. There

stood . . . Dorothy! Nancy looked so much like Dorothy that I gasped. She was wearing a white blouse and a blue-and-white-checked jumper. In her hand was a basket. But best of all, on her feet were pale blue socks and *sparkly ruby slippers!*

"Where did you get ruby slippers?" I asked. I was awed. Nancy was not wearing plain old red shoes or even red high heels that belonged to her mother. She had ruby slippers and they fit her.

"Mommy and Daddy ordered them from a catalog," she said. "They were a surprise for me. I just got them today."

"Come inside and show Andrew and my mother," I said.

So Nancy showed off her costume. Then she stayed to visit. While she was there, Ricky called.

"Guess what. I have straw for my Scarecrow costume," he said. "I am going to put it under my hat so that it sticks out."

Then David Michael called. "Daddy and Elizabeth bought me a *real* Lion costume!" he exclaimed.

Right after that, Hannie called. "Scott's costume is nearly finished," she told me. "He's got a funnel for his hat."

"Great," I said.

"And *I* am going to carry a bouquet of plastic flowers. That way, they will last forever. I am going to be an even more beautiful bride than I was at my wedding."

Ooh, this was so exciting! I could not *wait* until Saturday, when our whole group would be together. We were going to have the best costumes in the neighborhood, even if we did have a bride in the Land of Oz. Maybe no one would notice.

I had almost forgotten about Ben Brewer's haunted birthday party.

CHAPTER 14

Okay, class," said Ms. Colman with a big smile on her face. "*Now* you may change into your costumes."

It was Friday. My friends and I had been waiting all day for this moment. Party time! And time to show off our costumes and tell stories.

Waiting had been hard for me. In the morning, I forgot to raise my hand and talked out of turn *four times*. At reading I forgot to switch to my reading glasses. And I used my *out*door voice about a million times.

Oh, well. Ms. Colman had been very patient.

"Boys," our teacher continued, "take your things and go next door to Mr. Berger's classroom. You may change in there while his class is at recess. Girls, you stay here and change. I will wait in the hall. Call me if you need any help."

There was a big rush of excitement. When we girls were alone, we scrambled for our costumes. Most of them were in paper bags. I put on my witch outfit quickly. Then came the good part. I got to rub green goo on my hands and face, since the Wicked Witch of the West has green skin. Nancy helped me. (Hannie would not come near me because she did not want green goo on her white dress.)

Hannie and Nancy and I changed in a corner of the room with our backs to everyone. We kept grinning. We were having so much fun! Nancy waited until the last second to put on her ruby slippers.

Then we turned around. We planned to show Pamela a thing or two. But Pamela and her friends were ready for us. And just as Pamela had promised, they were wearing grown-up costumes.

Pamela was an airline stewardess. She was wearing a suit (the kind with a skirt) and stockings and even had wings pinned to her jacket. Jannie was dressed up like a punk rocker. She had sprayed her hair blue and made it all spiky. And she was wearing weird clothes. Leslie was standing with Pamela and Jannie. I knew she was one of the girls in our class who wanted to be cool Pamela's best friend. So I knew she had on a grown-up costume — but I was not sure what it was.

"What are you supposed to be?" Nancy asked Leslie.

"A waitress," Leslie replied proudly.

Suddenly I felt silly dressed as a witch. It *was* a baby costume. But then I looked around the room and saw a bunny rabbit and a Raggedy Ann and a princess. I felt better.

The door to our room opened then.

"How are you coming?" Ms. Colman asked us girls.

"We're ready!" I said.

In came the boys. I saw an athlete, a space creature, a cowboy, a policeman, some kind of animal, and finally . . . the Scarecrow!

Ricky stood with Hannie and Nancy and me and we could tell that the other kids were impressed. Except for Pamela, who said, "There's no bride in *The Wizard of Oz*."

When Ms. Colman wasn't looking, I made my most horrible face at Pamela.

The party began. Two room mothers came. They brought juice and cookies and candy corn. (I ate all my candy corn like this: white tip first, chocolate bottom second, orange part last.) We played two games. And then Ms. Colman said, "Okay, storytelling time."

"Ms. Colman! Ms. Colman!" I cried. "Can I tell my story last?"

I knew I had a *really* good story. I had not found the answers to my questions about Ben, but my story was true — and scary. I wanted to save it and surprise everyone.

CHAPTER 15

Ms. Colman said that I could tell my story last. Whew. I was going to be the hit of the party.

Here is what had happened with my story. I tried reading some more of Jeremy's diary, but it was hard. I could read it, but it took forever. So, maybe the true story of Ben Brewer *was* in the diary. If it was, though, I did not know it. Since I could not find the true story, I had decided to tell about the haunted birthday parties.

Ricky Torres was the first person to tell a scary story. That was because when Ms. Colman said, "Who would like to begin?" Ricky raised his hand really fast. He raised it so high, he practically stood up. And he said, "Ooh, ooh, ooh! Me, me, me!"

He told the story about the walking eye-balls.

Natalie Springer looked like she was going to throw up.

Five more people told stories. One of them was Pamela. Her story was stupid.

When nobody else had a story to tell, it was my turn. I stood up in front of the class and cleared my throat.

"In my house," I began, "we have a ghost."

Pamela rolled her eyes.

"His name is Ben Brewer, and he was my great-grandfather. His birthday was on . . . *Halloween*."

Natalie stared at me. She looked terrified.

Pamela yawned.

"Before Ben became a ghost himself," I continued, "he was haunted by *another* ghost."

Pamela look at her watch. I ignored her.

"Ben Brewer used to be just a normal person," I went on. "When he was young he got married. He and his wife had a baby. It was a boy, and they named him Jeremy. Jeremy was my grandfather."

"This is boring," I heard Pamela whisper to Natalie.

"Then something very sad happened," I said. "Ben's wife died. A few years later, Jeremy got married. So Ben was all alone in our big house. He became a recluse. He never left the house, except to get dandelions, so he could fry them and eat them. Then . . . one rainy night . . . Ben was sitting in his bedroom . . .

and the ghost appeared. He came down the chimney. Ben screamed."

(Natalie Springer screamed, too.)

The ghost said to Ben, "I am going to haunt you. I am going to haunt you for the rest of your life."

Pamela was staring at me. She had stopped whispering and fidgeting.

"Finally Ben grew very old, and he died, too," I said. "But he stayed in our house as a ghost. He decided that now he was going to give himself a haunted birthday party. But just once every ten years. He did not want to overdo things. So you know what happens on his birthday?" I went on. "This clock that never works chimes every hour . . ."

By this time, Pamela was looking very scared.

"And ghosts fly around the third floor, and you can hear the sounds of a party and smell a birthday cake baking."

Natalie began to cry. When she cries, she snorts. And the rest of the kids in my class looked terrified.

Ms. Colman said, "Well, Karen. Thank you very much."

I was not quite finished, but it was too late. The bell rang then. And *it* scared *me*. I jumped a mile. Pamela laughed. Still, it had been a very good party. And I had told a very scary story.

CHAPTER 16

That afternoon, as it was growing dark, Mommy drove Andrew and me to the big house. Our Halloween costumes were with us, of course. They were packed carefully in a box.

"Mommy? Do I *have* to go to Daddy's this weekend?" asked Andrew on the way.

"Yup," replied Mommy cheerfully. "We have talked about Karen's ghost story. You know there is nothing to be afraid of."

"I guess not," said Andrew, frowning.

But the next day, his frowns were gone. That was because all he could think about was going trick-or-treating. It was all Hannie and Nancy and David Michael and Scott and Ricky and

I could think about, too. (I am not sure about Emily Michelle.)

Just like the day before, the day of the Halloween party, we had to wait and wait and wait to put on our costumes. Kristy had said she would take us trick-or-treating at four o'clock. Around noon, I began looking at my costume. Andrew and David Michael looked at theirs, too. Finally, at two-thirty, we could not wait any longer. We got all dressed up. Then Kristy and I dressed Emily. Emily was a very cute Munchkin.

"People will give us *lots* of candy," said David Michael when he saw her.

At three-thirty, Hannie the bride came over. By a quarter to four, Ricky, Nancy, and Scott had arrived.

"Please can we go now, Kristy?" I begged. "We can't wait another second."

"Okay," said Kristy. But first Daddy and Elizabeth took about a million pictures of us. Then Hannie's parents came over and did the same thing.

When they were done, my friends and I ran across our front lawn. Our goody bags flopped against our sides.

"Wait for us!" called Kristy. She was holding Emily's hand. Emily is not a fast walker. "Slow down!" Kristy added.

The first house we went to was the house next door. *Not* Morbidda Destiny's — the house on the other side. We rang the bell. Mr. Giordano opened the door.

Before any one of us could say a word, Ricky the Scarecrow pushed his way to the front of our group. *"Trick or treat! Smell my feet! Give us something good to eat!"* he sang. *"If you don't —"*

"Ricky!" cried Kristy. "Stop that!"

Ricky stopped. And Mr. Giordano smiled. He's nice. He dropped a candy bar into each of our bags.

"See? The song works," said Ricky.

"Well, don't sing it again," Kristy told him. "It isn't polite."

Ricky calmed down. We walked from house to house to house. Almost everyone said what nice costumes we had. Our goody bags grew fuller and heavier.

And everyone *loved* Emily. One lady gave us two candy bars each when she saw her. David Michael nudged me. "Told you so," he said.

At last we had been to every house in our neighborhood — except Morbidda Destiny's.

"Are we going *there*?" squeaked Andrew, as I started up her driveway.

"Sure," I said.

"Why wouldn't we?" asked Ricky.

"It's a witch's house," I told him.

Ricky stopped. Everyone else stopped, too.

"Let's just go home," said Kristy.

"No," I replied. I ran to Morbidda Destiny's front door and rang the bell. No one answered. She wasn't home. I felt a little disappointed.

CHAPTER 17

I was sitting on the floor in my room. Trick-or-treating was over for another year. Hannie, Nancy, Ricky, and Scott had gone home.

I looked in my goody bag. Then I dumped it out. I counted up the candy bars first. Then I counted up the other things I'd gotten, like packages of peanuts and candy corn. Then I counted up the money. Some people had given us quarters! I had collected 75 cents. But the candy bars were best.

I wanted to eat a Milky Way bar. I wanted to eat one badly. (I had gotten three.) But Daddy and Elizabeth had said, "No candy until after dinner."

Instead, I took off my witch costume. As I

washed the green goo off of my hands and face, I thought of something. Ben Brewer.

Tonight would be his haunted birthday party. I'd been so excited about trick-or-treating that I had forgotten about Ben.

"Ooh," I said, and shivered.

Suddenly I was very, very scared. I left my costume and my candy (except for one of the Milky Way bars) in a mess on the floor.

I ran downstairs with the candy bar in my hand.

And I ran right into Charlie.

"Aughhh!" I screamed.

"Karen," said Charlie. "What's wrong? I was just about to call you for dinner. Has Halloween got you spooked?"

"Maybe," I said.

Charlie and I walked to the kitchen together. I sat at the table with my big-house family. When we had all been served, I said, "Tonight is Ben Brewer's haunted birthday party."

I guess no one heard me.

Emily said, "Candy!" loudly, and everyone laughed.

Then Nannie started talking about her bowling team. Sam pinched David Michael under the table. Daddy and Elizabeth kept getting up to answer the door when trick-or-treaters came. Kristy did not do anything but eat. She had been to a dance at school the night before. I think she has a b-o-y-f-r-i-e-n-d.

"Tonight is Ben's haunted party," I said again.

Even Andrew did not look very worried. "I will be asleep," was all he said.

I knew that I would be on my own that night. I would have to protect myself.

CHAPTER 18

When I went to bed on Halloween night, I just lay there. I clutched Moosie and Tickly in one arm. I clutched my goody bag in the other arm. Even though I had brushed my teeth, I could not help sneaking some candy every now and then.

The candy made me feel better. I could reach into the bag, find something small, like a root-beer barrel, and suck on it. The only problem was — then I wondered if I should get up to brush my teeth again.

No, I decided. No way. It was not midnight yet, but I was not going to take any chances. I would not want to run into a stray ghost. Who knew what time Ben's friends would start to arrive for the party?

I don't know when it happened, but some-time I fell asleep.

When I woke up, it was exactly midnight.

I lay in bed as stiff as a board. I could smell a *cake* baking! I could hear people laughing and talking! I think I could even hear horns blowing and party favors popping!

I was too scared to move or make any noise. I just lay in my bed. The next thing I knew, it was morning.

I had lived through a haunted birthday party.

I leaped out of bed. "Hurray!" I shouted. And that was when I saw it. Jeremy Brewer's diary. It was lying right on my bureau. It had not been there the night before. When I came to the big house for Halloween, I had asked Daddy to put the diary back in Ben's room. And now it was in *my* room.

I peered at the diary. It was open. And it was open to some pages that were stuck together. Very carefully, I unstuck them. Kristy could not have read these pages.

So I decided to.

I sat on my bed. I read the cursive slowly. (I was getting better at it.) Guess what? Somehow, Jeremy had learned the whole story, the *true* story, about his father. And this is the story:

When Ben was nine years old, he had had a fight with his best friend, Edward Porter. *Porter?* I thought. *Was Edward someone in Morbidda Destiny's family?* Anyway, during the fight, Ben told Edward that he couldn't come to his tenth birthday party. Right after the fight, Edward disappeared. He was never found. A lot of people thought he had drowned. That made sense, because Jeremy wrote that the ghost who haunted Ben was named Edward and he was always *wet*. (I had never heard that story.) Anyway, Edward haunted Ben because he was mad at him. He still wanted to go to the birthday party. And he told Ben that he would make Ben a ghost after he died.

Finally Ben did die. And Edward kept his promise to Ben. He made him a ghost. And he made him throw a ghost birthday party so that he could go and have fun. Now he makes Ben do that every ten years.

And that's the whole story.

I shivered. What an awful tale. I wanted that diary out of my room. Only this time I would get rid of it myself. I would put it back in Ben's room where it belonged — and I would check for any signs of a ghostly birthday party.

CHAPTER 19

I was gigundo scared as I walked up the stairs to the third floor. Below me, I could hear people talking. Nannie and Emily were probably up. So were Daddy and Elizabeth. I wished I could be with them. Instead, I walked down the hall. I stood by Ben's door.

Slowly, I opened it.

I expected to see balloons and cake crumbs and party favors.

But Ben's room looked just like it had when Kristy and I had explored it. (It felt damp, though.)

I put the diary back in the secret drawer in the table. I was about to stop and check *carefully* for anything — even a little piece of confetti — when I noticed the horrible thing.

The clock on the mantelpiece was *gone!*

The *clock!* When I told my scary story to Ms. Colman's class on Friday, I had made up the part about the clock that never worked, except on Ben's birthday.

And now the clock was gone.

I screamed.

Then I raced out of that haunted room and slammed the door behind me. I ran all the way downstairs to the first floor. I dashed into the kitchen. I was out of breath.

Daddy and Elizabeth and Nannie and Emily were there. Emily was in her high chair, eating toast.

"You guys! You guys! You won't believe this!" I cried.

"Karen, what's the matter?" Daddy wanted to know. "You look like you've seen a ghost. Try to calm down."

"I didn't see a ghost, Daddy," I said, "but I heard them. They've been here. And they had their party last night."

"What are you talking about?" asked Nannie. She sat me down. She put a bowl of cereal in front of me.

"I'm talking about Ben Brewer's haunted birthday," I said. "I told you about that yesterday. Kristy knows about it, too."

"Oh, Karen," said Daddy with a sigh. (Sometimes I make him sigh.)

"But I smelled a cake baking at *mid*night last night," I said.

"Honey, that was me," spoke up Elizabeth. "I couldn't sleep, so I baked a cake. It's in honor of Emily. She learned to count to ten."

Emily looked up and smiled. "One, two fee, four, five, sick, seben, eight, nine, ten!" she said proudly.

"But I heard a lot of noise then, too," I went on. "I heard laughing and talking and popping sounds."

"Those were some big kids in the neighborhood," said Daddy. "They were out late making Halloween mischief."

"Oh." I paused. "Well, there's one more thing. Ben's clock is missing. The one that was on his mantelpiece and didn't work."

"It's working now," said Daddy with a smile. "And it isn't missing. I had it fixed. It's in the living room."

"Okay," I said. "How did the diary get back in my room?" I told everyone how I had woken up and found the diary open to the story about Ben and Edward.

Before anyone could say anything, Sam came into the kitchen. He was grinning.

"*You* put the diary in my room last night!" I cried. "Didn't you?"

"What diary?" replied Sam. I could tell that he did not know what I was talking about. When Sam plays a joke on someone, he likes to brag about it.

Okay, I thought. *Maybe there was no party last night. But where did the diary come from?*

CHAPTER 20

That afternoon, Nancy's mother drove her over to the big house. Then Nancy and I went to Hannie's. The Three Musketeers were together.

We all had our Halloween candy with us, but none of us ate much. We'd eaten a lot of candy the night before. Especially me.

"Trick-or-treating was so, so fun, wasn't it?" said Hannie.

We were sitting on her back porch. Noodle the poodle was napping in the sun, and Myrtle the turtle was dozing in her box.

"It was gigundo fun," I said. "We should do the same thing next year. Only we should be characters from a different movie."

"Yeah," agreed Nancy. "Maybe *The Little Mermaid.*"

"How about *One Hundred and One Dalmations?*" said Hannie, giggling. "We would all be dalmations! . . . Except me. I think I will be a bride every Halloween. Or as long as Scott and I are married."

"I wonder how Pamela's Halloween was," I said. "I wonder if she is too grown-up to go trick-or-treating. Maybe she stays home and gives out the candy. If she does, I'm going to go to her house next year. And I will ring her bell and say, 'Trick or treat. Smell my feet.' And then I really *will* make her smell my feet!"

Hannie and Nancy and I laughed so loudly that we woke up Noodle. He left the porch looking grouchy.

"Well, I have some news," I said. I reached into my goody bag and pulled out a piece of Bazooka bubble gum. I unwrapped it and began chewing.

"What?" asked Hannie and Nancy together.

"I found out the *real* story of Ben Brewer. All of it."

"You *did?*" Hannie looked frightened.

I told my friends what had happened the night before. I told them about smelling the cake and hearing the noises. *Then* I told them about the clock. Of course, they were most interested in the diary and the story.

"How do you think the diary got into your room?" asked Nancy.

She asked it just as Hannie said, "I wonder if Morbidda Destiny is Edward Porter's niece. Or maybe even his younger sister."

"I don't know," I replied. "I don't know about either thing. The diary scares me more, though. I *know* Daddy put it away. And even if he didn't, I know it was *not* next to my bed when I went to sleep last night. Plus it was so weird. The diary was open to those stuck-together pages that told the story I'd been looking for. Even Kristy didn't find the story. It was almost as if . . . as if Ben Brewer wanted me to know what happened to him."

"Ooh," said Hannie and Nancy.

(I was glad Natalie Springer was not there. If she had been, she would have started crying and snorting.)

"I wonder if there really was a haunted party in your house last night," said Nancy.

"*I* wonder if there are really ghosts in my house," I said.

"I guess we'll never know," said Hannie.

"Well, at least you won't have to worry about a haunted birthday party for ten more years," Nancy pointed out.

"That's true," I replied. "And I'll be seventeen then. We all will be. Gosh, that's *Charlie's* age! I'll be a grown-up. Almost. Maybe I won't even believe in ghosts anymore. Charlie doesn't."

"You just never know," said Hannie again.

About the Author

Ann M. Martin's The Baby-sitters Club has sold over 190 million copies and inspired a generation of young readers. Her novels include the Newbery Honor Book *A Corner of the Universe*, *A Dog's Life*, and the Main Street series. She lives in upstate New York.

Keep reading for a sneak peek at the next
Baby-sitters Little Sister book!

Karen's Surprise

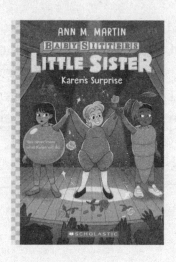

Karen! Dinner!" called Mommy.

"Coming!" I called back. I ran downstairs from my room. When Andrew and Mommy and Seth and I were sitting in the kitchen and had been served, I said, "Guess what."

"What?" asked everyone.

I could not believe that I had saved up the

news about our class play, but I had. I had not told anyone about it all afternoon. Now was the time. "Our class," I began importantly, "is going to put on a Thanksgiving play. We're going to put it on the day before Thanksgiving."

"That's wonderful!" exclaimed Seth.

"Terrific!" added Mommy.

"I'm sure I will have a big part in the play. Nancy, too," I said.

"When will you try out for it?" asked Seth.

"I don't know. Ms. Colman didn't say. I guess as soon as we know what the play will be about. I have to practice my acting. I can look sad, but Nancy can cry *real tears* — whenever she needs to. I bet she will get a bigger part than I will."

"Just do your best," said Mommy.

"I will," I told her. Then I asked, "Will you and Andrew and Seth *and* Daddy and Elizabeth and maybe Nannie and Emily Michelle come to the play? I really want you all to come and see me."

"We'll try," said Mommy. "I'm sure Seth and I can leave work for an hour or so during the day. Your father and Elizabeth probably can, too."

"Mommy?" spoke up Andrew. "Where are Karen and I going to have Thanksgiving?"

I saw Mommy and Seth look at each other. That is what adults do before they have to tell you something that they don't want to say.

"Well," replied Mommy, "this year everyone wants to celebrate Thanksgiving on Thursday."

"That's when you're supposed to celebrate it," I pointed out.

"Right," said Mommy. "And we all want you and Andrew to celebrate with us. Seth and I want you with us on Thursday, and so do your father and Elizabeth."

Hmm. That was a problem. "So what are we going to do?" I asked.

"You're going to have two Thanksgiving feasts on the same day. First you'll have dinner here. Then you'll go to Daddy's in the afternoon and eat another dinner."

"Two feasts!" I cried. "Two in one day! We'll be as stuffed as turkeys! We will be turkey stuffing!"

"I don't want to be turkey stuffing," said Andrew. He looked like he might cry.

"Don't worry. It will be fun," I told my brother. "I bet not many kids get to have two Thanksgivings in one day. That will be gigundo special."

"It will?" said Andrew.

"I'm sure it will."

After dinner, I was so excited about Thanksgiving that I wanted to tell my friends about it. I picked up the phone in the kitchen. I started to dial Nancy's number. Then I stopped. I did not want to talk to Nancy, and I knew why. I was a little bit mad at her. She could make herself cry, and I could not.

So I called Hannie instead.

"Guess what!" I said. "Andrew and I are going to have Thanksgiving at the little house and Thanksgiving at the big house — all in the same day."

"Karen, you are so lucky!" Hannie replied.

Don't miss any of the books in the Baby-sitters Little Sister series by Ann M. Martin—available as ebooks

Want more baby-sitting?

And many more!

DON'T MISS THE BABY-SITTERS LITTLE SISTER GRAPHIC NOVELS!